This book belongs

For Ella-May & Toby - K.R.
For Alex - A.N.

Bertie The Balloon at the Fairground first published by Kim Robinson and Aneta Neuman
This edition published 2015
Text copyright © Kim Robinson 2015
Illustrations © Aneta Neuman 2015

Printed in Poland
ISBN 978-0-9934627-0-2

Bertietheballoon@hotmail.com

Written by

Illustrated by

Kim Robinson

Aneta Neuman

Bertie The Balloon at the Fairground

Bertie is a BIG, red, shiny balloon.
He's round, squishy and shaped like the
MOON.

Bertie can fly high up in the sky,
Higher than the trees -
oh MY, oh MY!

How lucky that he is so light and free
As balloons are filled with air, you see.

But, be careful Bertie, don't get swept away.
The wind's a **DANGEROUS** place
for you to play.

Bertie has a secret he would like to share with you
Not only does he fly, but he can talk, too.

For Bertie is a MAGICAL balloon
Who goes on adventures, as you'll see soon.

Bertie lives at Fargo's Fairground
With Clancy the Clown, who is also
ROUND!

Clancy holds Bertie by a piece of string
Tied tightly around his finger, like a little ring.

The wind blew very hard and bold
And poor Clancy couldn't keep a hold.
Bertie's string snapped right in the middle
Up, up and away he climbed. "Oh FIDDLE."

Bertie screamed, "Clancy, please HELP ME!"

But it was too late; the clown could no longer see.

The wind was so incredibly strong.

It just kept blowing the balloon further on.

Backwards
and
forwards, up and down.

Bertie sailed so high he could see the whole town.
Onwards and upwards Bertie flew,
So high in the sky, such an AMAZING view.

Over the bumper cars and
under the slide
"Oh no, there's the haunted
house," said Bertie,
"I better hide."

Too late, the ghosts had already seen
"There's Bertie," they jeered.
"Let's go and be
MEAN."

BOOOO

They chased the balloon, quickening their pace,
But quick thinking Bertie pulled his UGLY face.

The ghosts got scared and flew back to their house.
After that, they were as quiet as a...

The wind pulled Bertie over the bandstand
where he saw two children walking hand in hand.

Drinking and eating, a hot dog for each.
"Can I have a BITE?" he asked,
but he couldn't reach.

All of a sudden the wind did dip
Blowing Bertie towards the roller coaster's tip.

Further and further, he dropped to the ground.
"OH NO!" Bertie screamed, going round and round.

Over big humps the carriages thundered
"When's this going to finish?"
Bertie wondered.

Turning green,
with his round head SPINNING,
"Oh, what's that?" he cried.
"I can hear a child singing."

Looking around, he could see a small boy
At the back of the roller coaster, his face full of joy.
"HELP ME?" said Bertie with a desperate look.
"Of course", said the boy. "Use your string as a hook."

Bertie pulled himself
towards the back
of the train
"Oh my," he puffed.
"What a terrible
S
T
R
A
I
N!"

With one last tug, he was almost there.
"No way," cried Bertie. "A tunnel, that's so unfair."

Into the tunnel the coaster swept.
"It's too **DARK** in here!" Bertie wept.

"Don't be sad," said a voice from nearby.
"I've got you now, please don't cry."

As Bertie opened his eyes, he could see
The little boy from the train, his face full of glee.

"THANK YOU for saving me from that terrible ride."
"That's ok. Come home with me?" Hugh replied.

"Oh yes, that would be wonderful," Bertie sang with JOY. "You can be my new owner," he told the little boy.

Now safe and secure with his brand new mate
"It's time for a new
ADVENTURE,"
Bertie cheered. 'And I can't wait!'

THE END

Can you spot Bertie ?

Bertie The Balloon at the Zoo

Bertie The Balloon at the Farm

Bertie The Balloon at the Seaside

Look out for more Bertie The Balloon adventures!